GARTH PIG
AND THE
ICE CREAM LADY

MARY RAYNER

M

MACMILLAN CHILDREN'S BOOKS

For Garth

First published 1977 by
MACMILLAN CHILDREN'S BOOKS
A division of Macmillan Publishers Limited
London and Basingstoke
Associated companies throughout the world

Picturemac edition published 1988

Reprinted 1991

British Library Cataloguing Publication Data
Rayner, Mary
    Garth Pig and the icecream lady.
    I.Title
    823'.914[J]

ISBN 0–333–47493–7

Printed in Hong Kong

One very hot day Mother Pig was washing the kitchen floor.

The ten piglets called Sorrel and Bryony and Hilary and Sarah and Cindy and Toby and Alun and William and Benjamin and Garth Pig were outside playing in the garden. They had made a fort and it had been very hard work. They were all tired and thirsty, when drifting across the neighbouring gardens they heard a faint *ting tong tingle tong*.

Dropping their guns and bows and arrows all over the grass, they ran squealing into the house to ask Mother Pig for icecream money.

"Mind the floor!" Mrs Pig cried. She searched for her handbag to find coins.

"All right, though it costs such a lot. Now don't all run into the road. One of you go and bring the ice-creams for the others."

"Your turn," said Toby to Alun.

"I got the arrows. It's William's turn," said Alun.

"Don't argue, or you'll miss the van," said Mrs Pig.

"Quick," said William. "Stand in a circle everyone,"
and he began to count round:

> *Ham, bacon, pork chop,*
> *Out you must hop.*

Mrs Pig held up her trotters in horror and turned away
her eyes. "Goodness me, where do they pick up such
words? I am sure they have never heard them in this
house."

But none of the piglets was listening. Round and round they counted until only Garth was left. With the money clenched tight in his trotter Garth ran as fast as he could out of the house.

"Ten Whooshes!" they called after him.

The van was parked down the road. It was a pink and brown *Volfswagon*, and written across the side in fat curly letters was *Lupino's Icecreams*.

SINGLE CONE 9P
DOUBLE TOP CONE 20P
WHOOSH 8P
MOONLIGHT MINT 15P
FOREST SPECIAL 15P
WOODFOLK'S
WONDERBAR 15P

ICECREAM
CONES

DOUBLE
CONE
20P

NO
MS

The window slid open,
a paw appeared over the
counter and a face smiled
fondly down at Garth.
Garth was counting the
money to see what
would be left after nine
Whooshes. He was
hoping there might be
enough over for a
double cone with
chocolate flakes on top
for himself.

"Nine Whooshes," he
said, "and – and – "

"Why don't you come up into the van, my dear,"
said the icecream lady, "and see what's in the freezer?"

Garth trotted up the step and into the van. As he
leaned over the freezer the icecream lady closed the
door and slipped behind the driving wheel. The van
began to move. It lurched off up the road carrying
Garth Pig with it.

Meanwhile in the back garden the nine piglets were lying about on the grass waiting for their icecreams.

"He is being a long time," said Sarah Pig.

"Probably dropped them," said William unkindly.

"Silly little pig," said Alun.

"Maybe he's eating them," said Toby.

The piglets looked at each other. It was a worrying thought.

"Better go and see," said Hilary.

They streamed in through the back door. Mrs Pig had almost finished scrubbing.

"Mind the floor," she said.

"But Mum, we're in a hurry," said Sorrel as they ran past, out of the front door and into the road.

There was no Garth. No van either. Just a few blobs of icecream in a trail up the road. The piglets stood open-mouthed.

"He's been taken," said Sorrel. "Come on everyone, the bicycle."

Together they ran to the garage. Leaping onto the bicycle they swung out into the road and pedalled along the icecream trail.

But they had not gone far when they came to a cross-roads. There the spots of icecream petered out. The piglets came to a stop.

"Have you seen an icecream van that goes *ting tong tingle tong*?" they asked a passer-by.

"No," she answered, "but one did go by which was going *snort squeal grunt grunt*. It went that way," and she pointed.

Far ahead the icecream van had crossed the bridge and was climbing the long steep hill the other side, heading for the forest.

Inside the van the driver
was singing softly to
herself:
*Fried or boiled, baked or
roast,
Or minced with mushey-
rooms on toast?*

Garth Pig heard her.
It was not a song about
icecream.

The road climbed up and up. The van was going slower and slower, and the icecream lady stopped singing. There was a nasty smell of burning and the engine was making an odd uneven chugging. Then it stopped. The icecream lady left her seat and got out to look, but she locked the door behind her.

Trapped inside, Garth
Pig stood on tiptoe and
pressed his snout to the
window. It was very hot
in the van. He peered
with his little pig eyes
down the steep grassy
slope of the hill, and far
far away at the bottom,
tiny in the distance, he
saw the family bicycle
toiling bravely up the
road.

Then he caught sight of the icecream lady coming back round to the door. He held his breath and ducked down. Now or never, he thought, watching the door handle turn.

As the door opened he bolted past her, dodged round the van, and with a piercing squeal flung himself down the hillside.

Down the steep slope he rolled, as round and as smooth as a barrel, gathering speed as he went.

The other nine piglets heard the squeal and saw him bowling down towards them. Nearer and nearer he came . . .

shot past and down and with a huge bounce came to rest in some bushes near the bottom of the hill. With one accord his brothers and sisters dropped the bicycle and ran back down after him.

William picked him out of the prickles and the others gathered round. He was sobbing, "It's not an icecream lady it's – " when they heard a terrible howl.

The bicycle streaked
down the hill, a frantic
figure clinging to the
handlebars. The icecream
lady had snatched up their
bike. But that bike was
made to fit ten piglets,
not one lone wolf, and it
hurtled past them . . .

swerved round the bend at the bottom and hit the
parapet of the bridge. A dark shape sailed over the
handlebars and fell with a tremendous splash into the
river.

The piglets looked at the water. There was no sign of anyone. They looked up the hill to where the van still stood.

"We still haven't had our Whooshes," said Sorrel. They scampered up the hill, Garth trailing after them. "Don't want a Whoosh, want a double cone," he whimpered.

Sorrel opened the van door and went to the freezer. She handed out nine Whooshes, but when it came to Garth she paused.

"Here," she said, "there was enough money, I know there was."

She scooped out two gloriously over-flowing cones and putting a fat chocolate flake in each, gave it to him.

Then they all ran down the hill, picked up the bicycle, straightened the handlebars and rode home.

Next morning the van was gone from the hilltop, but Madam Lupino was not heard of again for a very long time.